the Bastard
★★★ PHOTOSTORY™

Adapted from MCA/UNIVERSAL's glittering television drama, THE BASTARD, this Photostory™ unfolds in pictures the bold saga of Philip Kent—his high adventures in a wild new nation and the passion that seeded a dynasty.

It is the saga, too, of a young America, struggling to be free, and of the proud men and women who gave it life...

CAST

Starring

ANDREW STEVENS as........ Phillipe Charboneau/
Philip Kent

and
Guest Starring (alphabetically)

NOAH BEERY	Dan O'Brian
PETER BONERZ	Girard
TOM BOSLEY	Benjamin Franklin
KIM CATTRALL	Anne Ware
JOHN COLICOS	Lord North
WILLIAM DANIELS	Samuel Adams
BUDDY EBSEN	Benjamin Edes
LORNE GREENE	Bishop Francis
JAMES GREGORY	Will Campbell
OLIVIA HUSSEY	Alicia
HERBERT JEFFERSON, JR.	Lucas
CAMERON MITCHELL	Capt. Plummer
HARRY MORGAN	Capt. Caleb
PATRICIA NEAL	Marie Charboneau
ELEANOR PARKER	Lady Amberly
DONALD PLEASENCE	Solomon Sholto
WILLIAM SHATNER	Paul Revere
BARRY SULLIVAN	Abraham Ware
KEENAN WYNN	Johnny Malcolm

A JOVE BOOK

the Bastard
PHOTOSTORY™

Executive Producer	
Producer	Joe Byrne
Director	Lee H. Katzin
Television Adaptation	John Wilder
Teleplay	Guerdon Trueblood
Director of Photography	Michel Hugo
Art Director	Loyd Papez
Set Decorator	Richard Friedman
Music	John Addison
Editors	Bob Shugrue & Michael Murphy
Makeup	Tony Lane
Costumes	Vincent Dee & Jean Pierre Dorleac
Production Manager	Fred Simpson
Associate Producer	Susan Lichtwardt

Photostory™ produced by Lyle Kenyon Engel

Copyright © 1980 by John Jakes and Book Creations, Inc. Photographs from the television series entitled THE BASTARD, copyright © Universal City Studios, Inc. MCMLXXVIII. All rights reserved.

Layout by Flash Graphics

First Jove edition published February 1980

All rights reserved. No part of this publication may be reproduced or transmitted in any form or by any means, electronic or mechanical, including photocopy, recording, or any information storage and retrieval system, without permission in writing from the publisher.

Requests for permission to make copies of any part of the work should be mailed to Jove Publications, Inc., 200 Madison Avenue, New York, N.Y. 10016

Printed in United States of America

10   9   8   7   6   5   4   3   2   1

Jove books are published by
Jove Publications, Inc., 200 Madison Avenue,
New York, N.Y. 10016

His name was Phillipe Charboneau . . . and he was born a bastard. His home was in the French countryside, but his heritage would call him down a high road of adventure . . . adventure for which he was bred. A destiny to which he was born.

He was a man like so many others who came before him, and after . . . a man coming to America to become an American.

the Bastard
PHOTOSTORY™

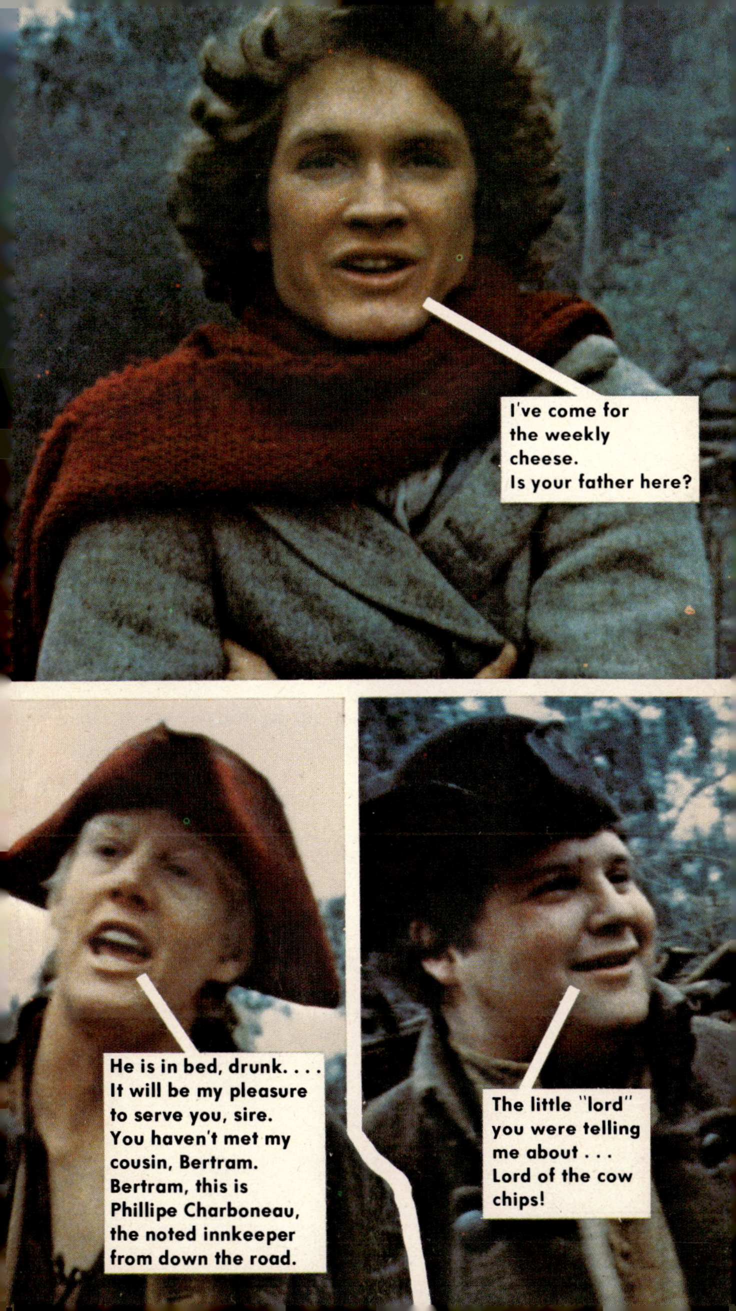

My poor Phillipe . . . Here, you need a little wine.
Where did you get the wine? From the store-room? Who gets the rest of what you steal?
I drink it all. And have the loveliest dreams of a certain young man. . . . And oh, they are lovely. What a pity they stay dreams and nothing else!
Love warms the blood . . . unless you hurt too much?
Charlotte, I've been beaten stoutly. I don't think we . . .
If my mother finds us . . .
She won't, she won't. . . .

Marie enters the stable and finds Phillipe and Charlotte...

My God! Did she rake you like that?... Go inside, Charlotte, and tell Girard he is to give you wages for the week and escort you home. Don't come back.

Why? Because I've had *him*? I'm not good enough for your precious little lord? I'm not good enough when *he* is a bastard and *you* can't even get past a church door because...

You will leave!

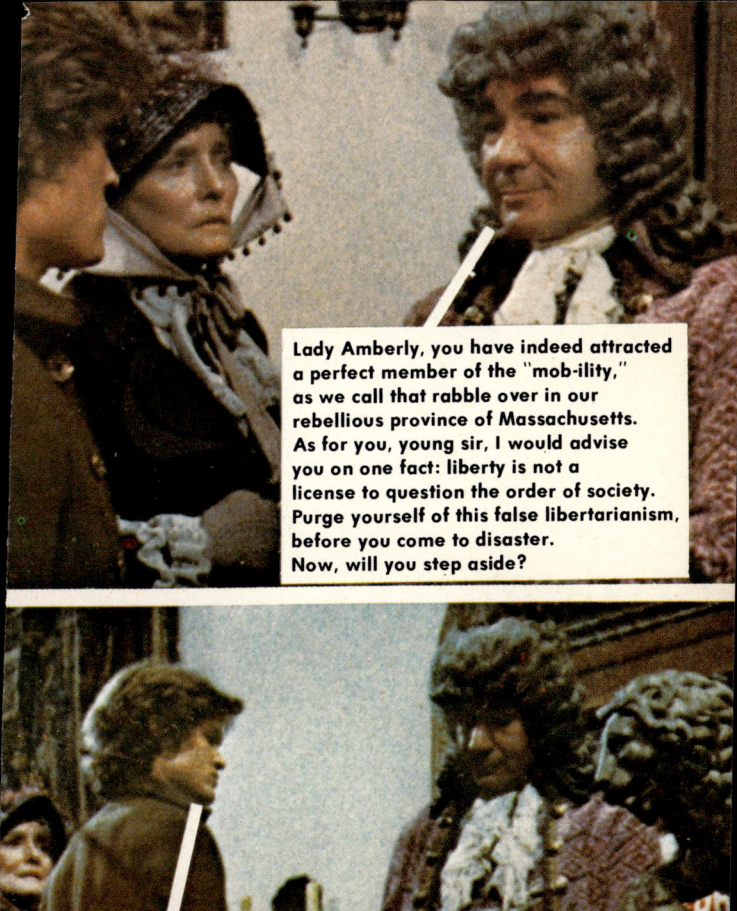

Lady Amberly, you have indeed attracted a perfect member of the "mob-ility," as we call that rabble over in our rebellious province of Massachusetts. As for you, young sir, I would advise you on one fact: liberty is not a license to question the order of society. Purge yourself of this false libertarianism, before you come to disaster. Now, will you step aside?

Take a good look, Mama. That is what you wanted me to be. Perhaps Girard was right, after all.

"This household is in mourning. Have you no respect?"

"Let me in."

"Madame, you exceed the bounds of all decency. Leave at once. My husband, before he died, woke and charged me to care for our son — his legitimate son. You have no claim on us. The matter is closed."

"You French scum!"

Marie moves forward, but Roger, enraged, steps in her way and throws her to the floor.

As Phillipe rushes to his mother's aid, Roger attacks him with his cane.

I'll kill you. For tormenting my mother, seducing my fiancee. She flaunted you — her French *lover!* French *bastard!*

Roger moves quickly at the dazed Phillipe, jamming the cane . . .

. . . against his throat and choking him.

Phillipe breaks Roger's stranglehold, seizes his cane...

...and begins to beat Roger. As Roger tries to resist, his hand is struck several times.

Phillipe realizes what he is doing, and ceases. Roger is left on the stairs, stunned, his hand severely injured.

God help me, what have I done?

Come, Mama!

"Let them go. See to my son, do you hear? See to my son!"

Roger calls to Plummer, a hired bodyguard and assassin.

"I want his head, Plummer. A thousand pounds when you bring it to me — in a basket!"

Phillipe and Marie flee, knowing they can never return to Kentland.

Phillipe and his mother, bound for London, are overtaken by a rider. Alicia.

"You're right to leave, Phillipe. Dr. Bleeker says he can't save Roger's hand. If he ever sees you again, Roger will kill you."

"Come with me, Alicia. I don't care about Kentland. I want you!"

"And I want you. I'll always feel you close, even when I'm with another man, for all the rest of my life."

"But you won't come with me?"

To where? Oblivion?

Goodbye, Alicia.

A saddened Alicia stands alone. That night, the Charboneaus reach their destination: London, glittering and swarming with humanity. Penniless, they seek refuge on the grounds of St. Paul's Cathedral, where they are surrounded by beggars and thieves.

At first vigilant, Phillipe at length dozes off... until he is startled by a scuffling sound.

He draws his sword as a band of beggars, intent on mischief, approach with stealth.

Hah! We caught ourselves a Frenchified rat what swum the Channel. We'll have that sword and her jewel box, too.

Get away! I said, get away!

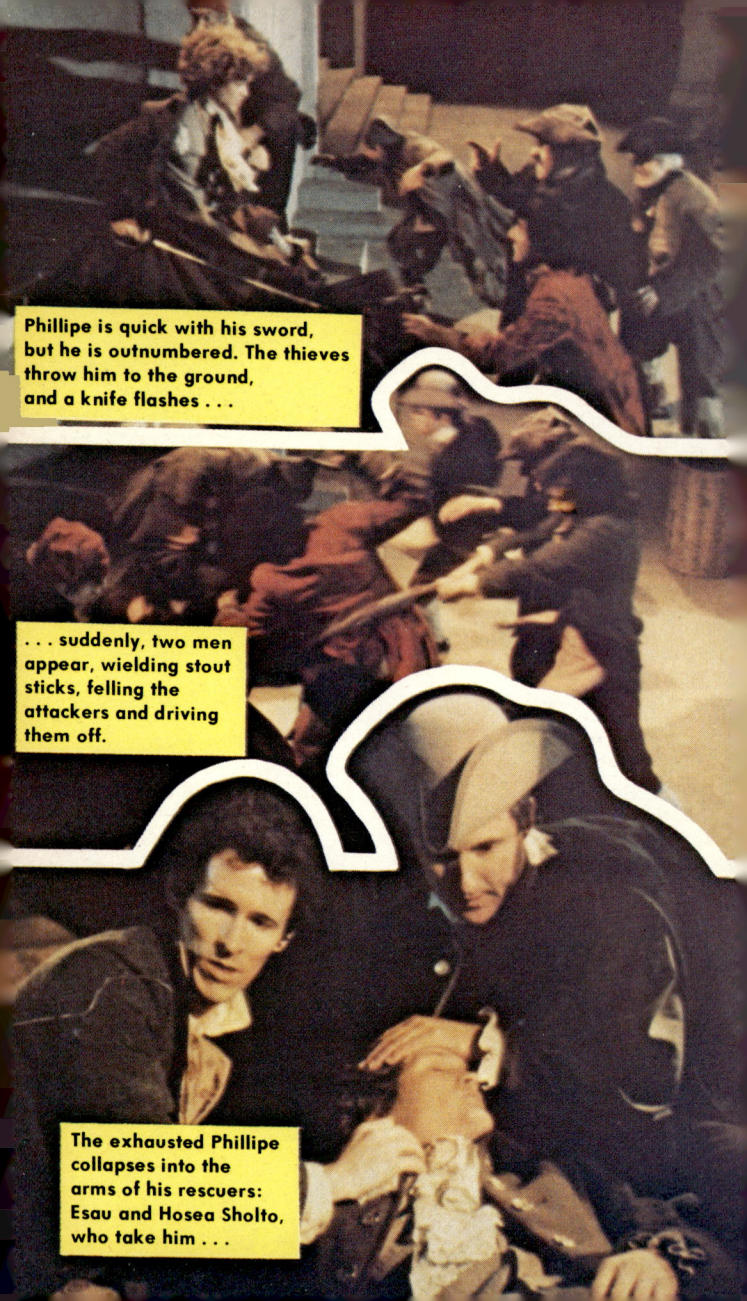

Phillipe is quick with his sword, but he is outnumbered. The thieves throw him to the ground, and a knife flashes...

...suddenly, two men appear, wielding stout sticks, felling the attackers and driving them off.

The exhausted Phillipe collapses into the arms of his rescuers: Esau and Hosea Sholto, who take him...

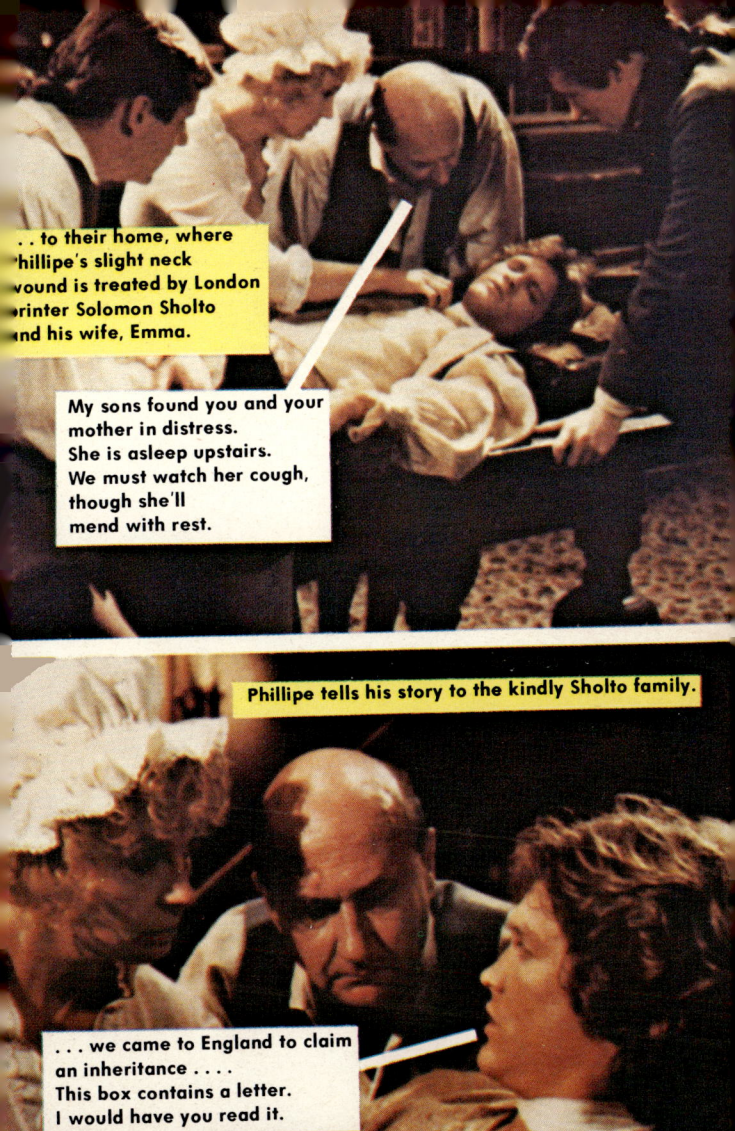

...to their home, where Phillipe's slight neck wound is treated by London printer Solomon Sholto and his wife, Emma.

My sons found you and your mother in distress. She is asleep upstairs. We must watch her cough, though she'll mend with rest.

Phillipe tells his story to the kindly Sholto family.

...we came to England to claim an inheritance.... This box contains a letter. I would have you read it.

Sholto reads the letter, then offers Phillipe a haven in his home until his mother recovers.

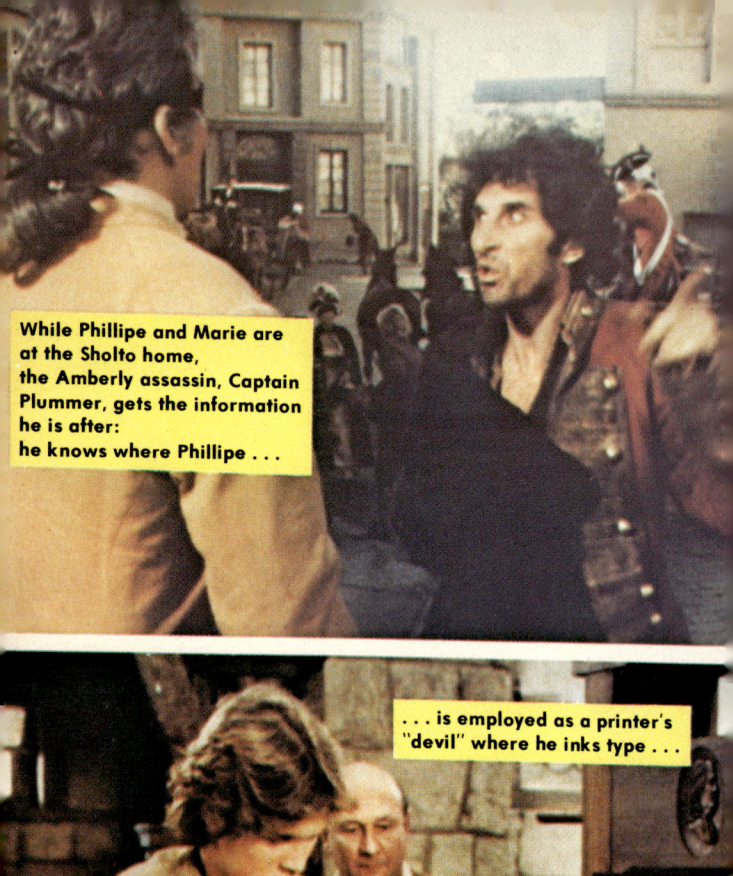

While Phillipe and Marie are at the Sholto home, the Amberly assassin, Captain Plummer, gets the information he is after: he knows where Phillipe...

...is employed as a printer's "devil" where he inks type...

...and learns the printer's trade. Sholto takes a liking to the young Frenchman, and one day invites Phillipe to meet a visitor.

Phillipe, I promised to introduce you to a colonial. It is your good fortune to meet one of such eminence. Dr. Benjamin Franklin.

Sholto tells Franklin that Phillipe would like a copy of the Philadelphian's "Observations Concerning the Increase of Mankind."

Then come to my lodgings, young man, and the book shall be yours. But may I ask the reason for your interest?

"Well, it... it's the New World, sir."

"Aye. And if you should be thinking of going there, the opportunities are unlimited, particularly for an ambitious boy who can ply a press. I would be glad to provide you with a letter of recommendation to some first-class printing houses. We can discuss it further when you call."

Marie wants Phillipe to think about Kentland, not about the New World.

"And you, Solomon, we'll expect you at the Turk's Head, where the Whig Party is coming to life again over coffee cups! Good day to you all!"

A few nights later, Phillipe is leaving Sholto's to visit Dr. Franklin, when Marie stops him.

How can you entertain the idea of another country when your position is right here in England?

Kentland? Oh, Mama, let it die!

You swore an oath! You [ar]e a nobleman, not a [tr]adesman! I've been hoarding [m]y money.... We'll find [a] lawyer in London....

Yes, Mama. Now, I'm going to see Dr. Franklin only because he's a great man. I'm flattered, that's all.

As he leaves, he is watched by the lurking Plummer, who follows him.

Phillipe arrives at Franklin's apartments on Craven Street, where a maid shows him in.

He's having his air bath. Dr. Franklin, you have a visitor.

Ah, Charboneau, good of you to come! Have a chair. Help yourself to that Madiera, I'll be finished with my air bath in just a few minutes.

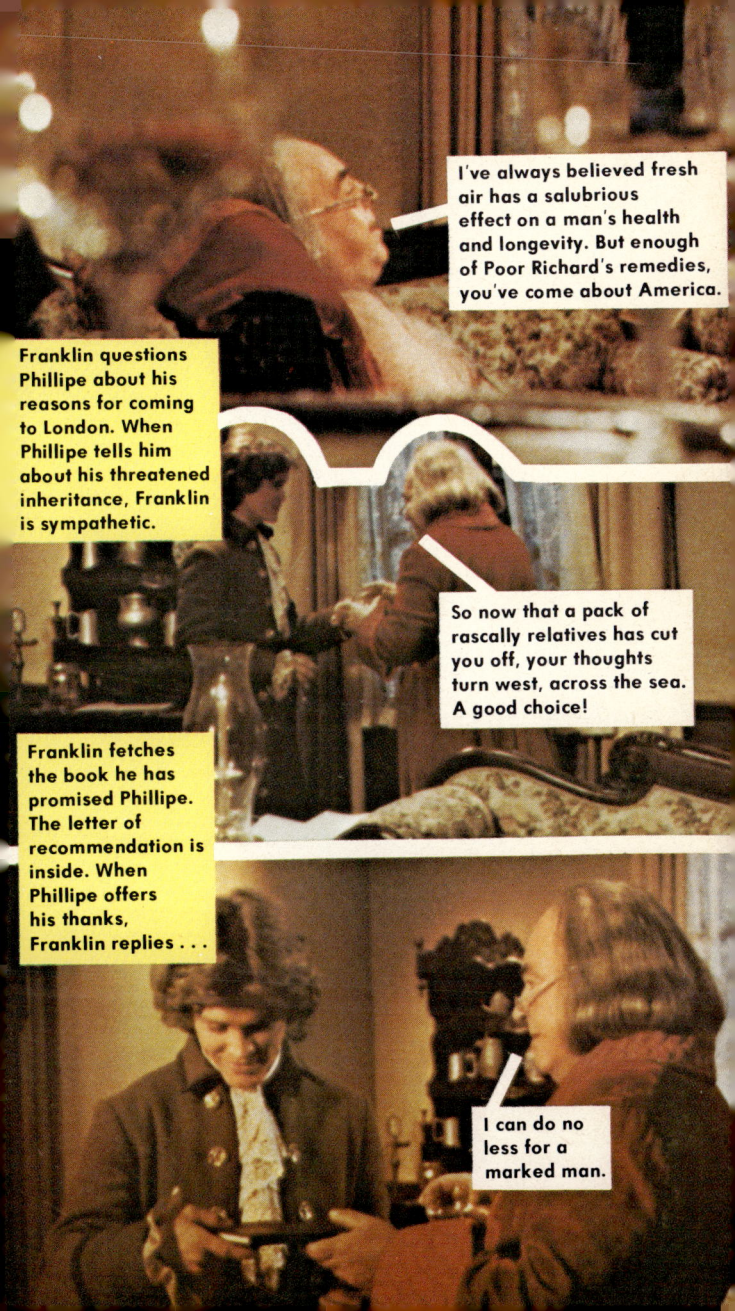

"I've always believed fresh air has a salubrious effect on a man's health and longevity. But enough of Poor Richard's remedies, you've come about America."

Franklin questions Phillipe about his reasons for coming to London. When Phillipe tells him about his threatened inheritance, Franklin is sympathetic.

"So now that a pack of rascally relatives has cut you off, your thoughts turn west, across the sea. A good choice!"

Franklin fetches the book he has promised Phillipe. The letter of recommendation is inside. When Phillipe offers his thanks, Franklin replies...

"I can do no less for a marked man."

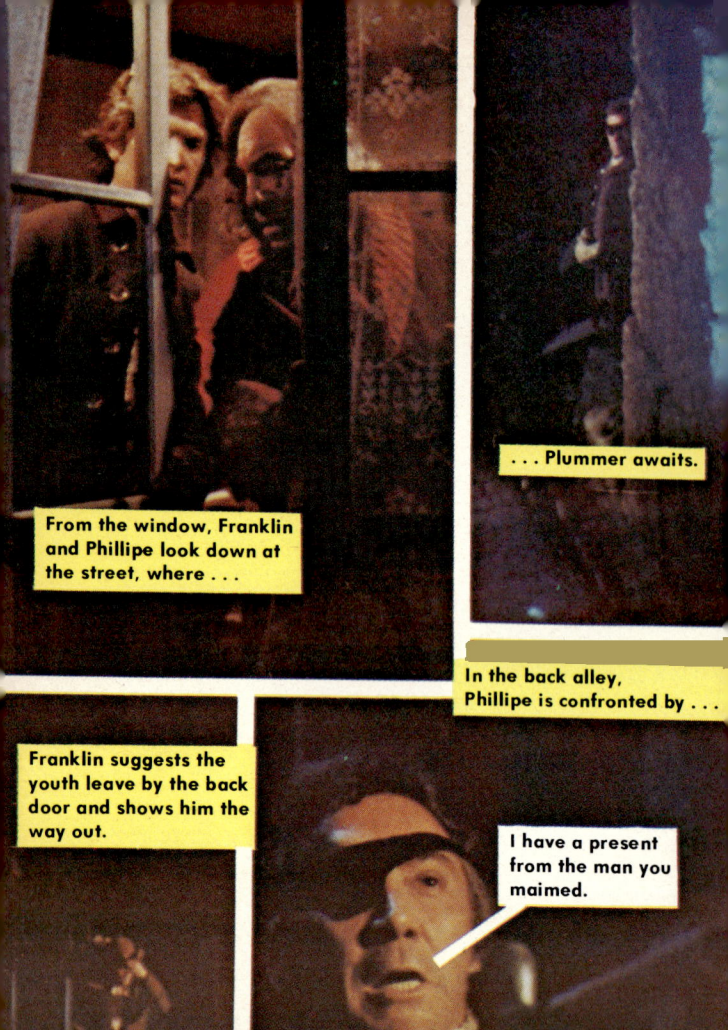

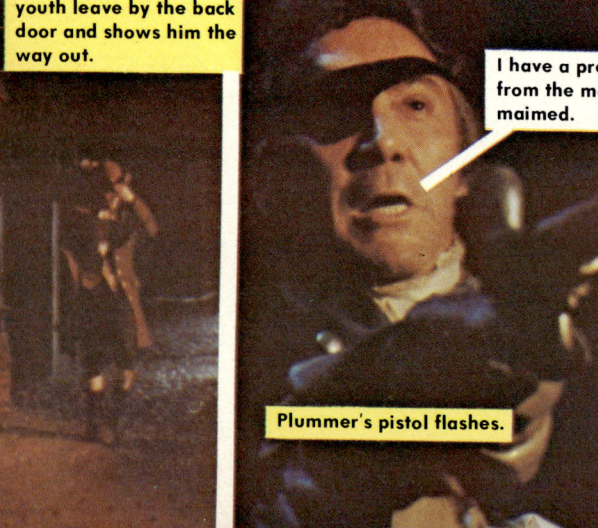

From the window, Franklin and Phillipe look down at the street, where...

...Plummer awaits.

Franklin suggests the youth leave by the back door and shows him the way out.

In the back alley, Phillipe is confronted by...

I have a present from the man you maimed.

Plummer's pistol flashes.

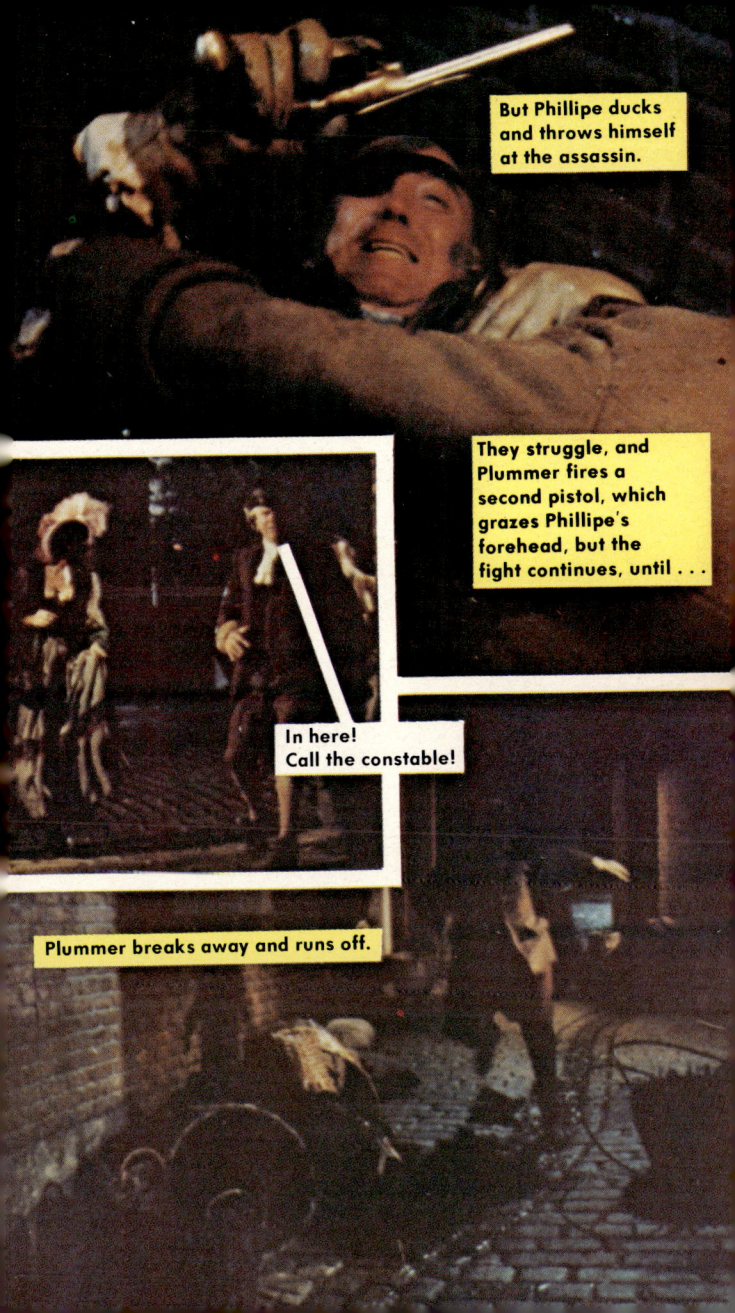

But Phillipe ducks and throws himself at the assassin.

They struggle, and Plummer fires a second pistol, which grazes Phillipe's forehead, but the fight continues, until . . .

In here! Call the constable!

Plummer breaks away and runs off.

At the Sholto home, Phillipe's slight wound is treated.

He was hired by the Amberlys.

The very fact they sought you proves they fear your claim.

They can strike down any claim by manipulating the law. It's me Roger wanted, in payment for what I did to his hand. Even if I'd killed this one-eyed assassin, he'd send another and another until the job was done. We'll have to leave London.

I know. We'll go in the other direction. To the colonies.

If they anticipate your flight, they'll be watching the Channel ports, any passage back to France.

Never! I won't go! I won't.

Mama, it's my life they're after. If you want me here, you want me dead.

Reluctantly, Marie agrees to go with Phillipe.

The next morning a coach races toward the seaport city of Bristol. Marie is inside and...

...perched atop the coach, Phillipe is alerted by a Blackamoor named Lucas that riders are approaching the coach.

Warning shots are fired, and the coach draws to a halt. The highwaymen are led by...

"Captain Plummer, at your service. Drag out the passengers!"

Plummer's two accomplices herd the frightened passengers together, and Marie is hauled roughly from the coach.

Infuriated, Phillipe hurls himself down onto the highwayman.

Plummer quickly fires, but . . .

... Phillipe wrenches his opponent into the path of the ball.

Lucas whips up the coach guard's blunderbuss and blasts the second highwayman. He leaps at Plummer, whose rearing horse prevents him from drawing his second pistol.

Plummer throws Lucas off and reaches for the weapon, intent on killing Phillipe.

But Phillipe snatches a pistol from the dead highwayman near him and fires.

Plummer slumps backwards, dead.

Phillipe and Marie reach the seaport.

Bristol, England

At a waterfront tavern, Phillipe meets Captain Will Caleb, a no-nonsense New Englander who knows Phillipe cannot pay the usual passage to the New World. But the sympathetic captain offers to take them if Phillipe will work in the galley.

The merchantman Eclipse is underway far out in the Atlantic. Phillipe is excited about the prospects of starting a new life. But Marie, who is suffering from melancholy and a worsening cough, is grim and sickly.

No... I can't... Phillipe, help me.

Mama, Mama, you have to hold on.

As the days drag into weeks, Marie is confined by illness to her cabin. Phillipe carves a wooden cross for her.

Marie awakens with a cry.

Phillipe!

Here, Mama, I've been making you something.

He presses the cross into her withered hands.

I will never reach this America of yours.

Mama, don't say that. You must eat. You have to help yourself live.

what purpose? erything I held out hope for you... t you made the ht decision, illipe. You're ung. You've done right thing. ce I made you swear oath, but you st forget that. ow only beg from u a promise...

That in this new land you will strive to be a man of position, a man of wealth. Then someday you can repay them. Repay them! Damn their arrogant souls!

Marie falls back, only half conscious. A heartsick Phillipe gazes at her, helplessly.

I promise Mama... I promise.

In the morning, the <u>Eclipse</u> reefs sail and pauses on its journey. Marie Charboneau is dead. While Phillipe and the crewmen look on, Captain Caleb reads from the Bible over the canvas-wrapped body.

Let not your heart be troubled . . . I go to prepare a place for you. And I will come again and receive you . . . .

The weighted canvas slips silently from the tilted board and swishes into the sea.

The Eclipse hoists sail and catches a fresh wind once more, her course set for America. Phillipe confides in Captain Caleb, showing him the Amberly letter.

It's my opinion that this letter is as binding as one could be in a civilized world. Not that you could ever enforce it. But your half brother can never rest until he knows this is destroyed. I suggest a final separation from this ugly past. Why not start as a new man entirely? With a new identity. A new name.

While Phillipe ponders Captain Caleb's advice, there is a cry from above in the rigging.

Land ho!

America! On the hazy horizon, the new world is at last in sight.

I've crossed more than fifty times. But it always gives me a shiver.

> Phillipe gazes at the vision of the new land awaiting him. As he wonders about his future, he mutters his name... his new name.

> Phillipe Kent...
> Philip Kent...
> Philip Kent...

> And the Eclipse, under full canvas, sails on into Nantucket Roads and a new world.

Philip Kent arrives in Boston, the greatest seaport city in the New World. The teeming waterfront throbs with the babble of busy people.

His search for work is futile.

I'm sorry. I wish I knew of something for you.

I don't know of anybody looking for help. Times are bad.

Rejection and discouragement greet Philip at every turn. His eagerness is blunted as his hunger grows. He is penniless, alone in a seemingly hostile city.

The desperation of a starving man leads Philip to scrounge in the garbage of an alleyway. As a handy weapon, he slips a sharp clamshell into his pocket.

An exhausted Philip stumbles into two English officers, splashing mud on them.

Damn! The clumsy oaf dirtied my trousers.

Then we shall make him pay for a laundress, Captain.

You! Come round to the headquarters of the Fourteenth West Yorkshires in the morning, and . . .

Philip sullenly pushes the officer away and backs off. The arrogant Lieutenant Stark draws his sword.

As you wish.

He's probably sporting a liberty medal under those clothes. He's insolent enough to be one of them. Do I have permission to thin their ranks somewhat, Captain.

As Stark circles, his sword taunting, Philip slips the jagged clamshell from his pocket.

Before the officer can strike, Philip leaps at him and rakes his face with the shell.

Howling in pain, Stark recoils, a deep gash on his handsome face.

The captain reaches for his sword when a voice barks...

Stay your hand! You've made one mistake. No need to make another.

At the head of an angry crowd of Bostonians, Will Campbell, proprietor of the nearby inn, <u>The Salutation</u>, confronts the officers, a half-drawn sword in hand.

The desperation of a starving man leads Philip to scrounge in the garbage of an alleyway. As a handy weapon, he slips a sharp clamshell into his pocket.

An exhausted Philip stumbles into two English officers, splashing mud on them.

Damn! The clumsy oaf dirtied my trousers.

Then we shall make him pay for a laundress, Captain.

You! Come round to the headquarters of the Fourteenth West Yorkshires in the morning, and . . .

Philip sullenly pushes the officer away and backs off. The arrogant Lieutenant Stark draws his sword.

As you wish.

He's probably sporting a liberty medal under those clothes. He's insolent enough to be one of them. Do I have permission to thin their ranks somewhat, Captain.

As Stark circles, his sword taunting, Philip slips the jagged clamshell from his pocket.

Before the officer can strike, Philip leaps at him and rakes his face with the shell.

Howling in pain, Stark recoils, a deep gash on his handsome face.

SALUTATION

Stay your hand! You've made one mistake. No need to make another.

The captain reaches for his sword when a voice barks...

At the head of an angry crowd of Bostonians, Will Campbell, proprietor of the nearby inn, <u>The Salutation</u>, confronts the officers, a half-drawn sword in hand.

"Move aside, sir! You see what he's done to my face!"

"The initiative is out of Philip's hands."

"Improved it considerably. I would remind you where you are, gentlemen. If you truly wish to engage, I can guarantee that a substantial part of the North End will be after your heads before three blows are struck."

"Leave off, Stark, or you'll have a cut across your throat to match the one on your face."

"One of these days we'll have laws permitting us to hang you rebel scum!"

"There'll be hangings, all right. But it will be your necks, stretched under the Liberty Tree."

The furious officers push their way through the surly mob, as shouts of assent are followed by an offer from Campbell of free drinks in the tavern.

The grateful Philip is served food in honor of his courage in standing up to the despised Redcoat officers. The talk turns quickly to Philip's need for work to earn his keep, and he tells of his apprenticeship to the Sholtos.

His words catch the ear of Benjamin Edes, himself a printer.

I'll take this one off your hands, Will... if, indeed, he is a printer!

With everything at stake Philip feverishly plies the press in the printing house. The sober Edes looks closely at Philip's work and likes what he sees.

You can sleep on a cot in the back. But there's hard work here.

And dangerous work, judging by these words. The Gazette, what is it, sir?

A voice of dissent, written by Samuel Adams, a leader of what the Tories call the "mob-ility."

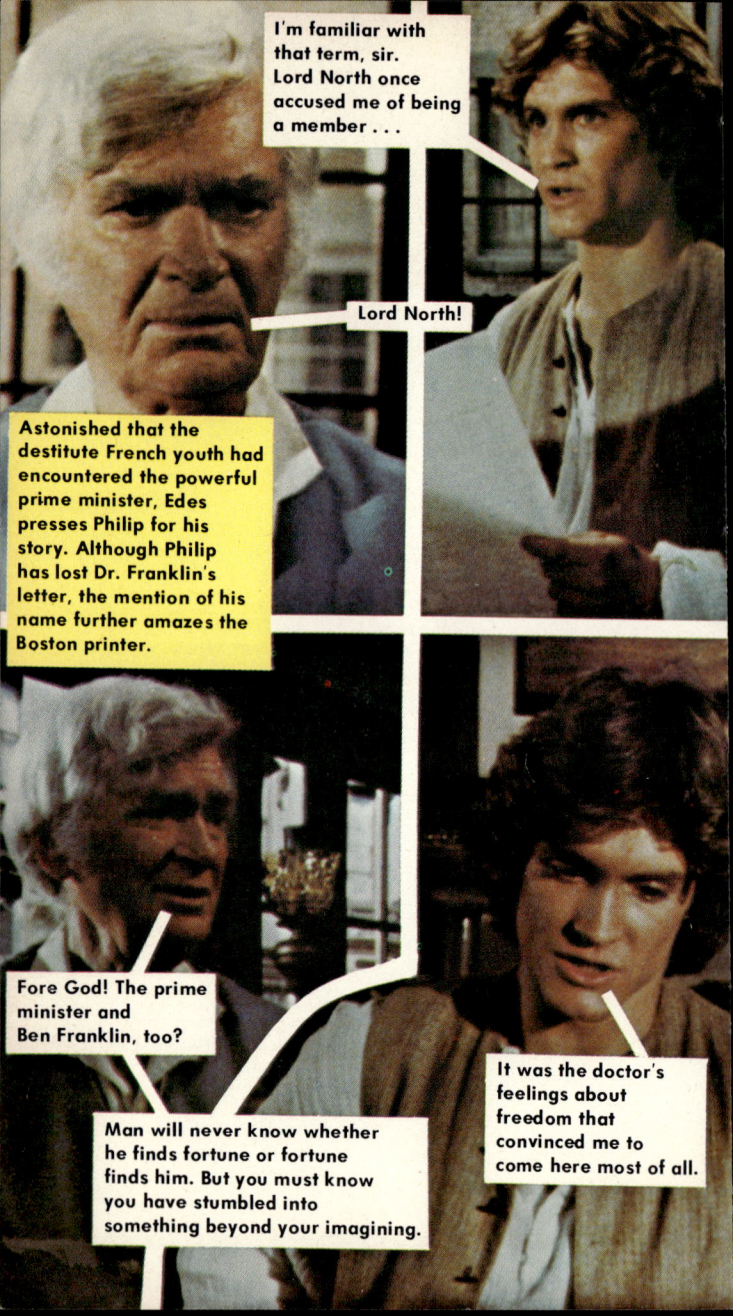

"I'm familiar with that term, sir. Lord North once accused me of being a member..."

"Lord North!"

Astonished that the destitute French youth had encountered the powerful prime minister, Edes presses Philip for his story. Although Philip has lost Dr. Franklin's letter, the mention of his name further amazes the Boston printer.

"Fore God! The prime minister and Ben Franklin, too?"

"Man will never know whether he finds fortune or fortune finds him. But you must know you have stumbled into something beyond your imagining."

"It was the doctor's feelings about freedom that convinced me to come here most of all."

...des removes a silver medal from around his neck and hands it to Philip. It is the Liberty Medal worn by members of the Sons of Liberty, the secret group that opposes British oppression of the American colonies.

"Our purpose is the guarantee of liberty. There's great risk here, son. Are you prepared to accept it?"

"Yes, sir."

The two men step into the street, where they hear a crowd shouting "Tar and feathers!"

"Who is that?"

"Old Johnny Malcolm, a harmless lunatic."

A clattering cart approaches bearing a trussed-up old man who is hurling wild insults at the mob.

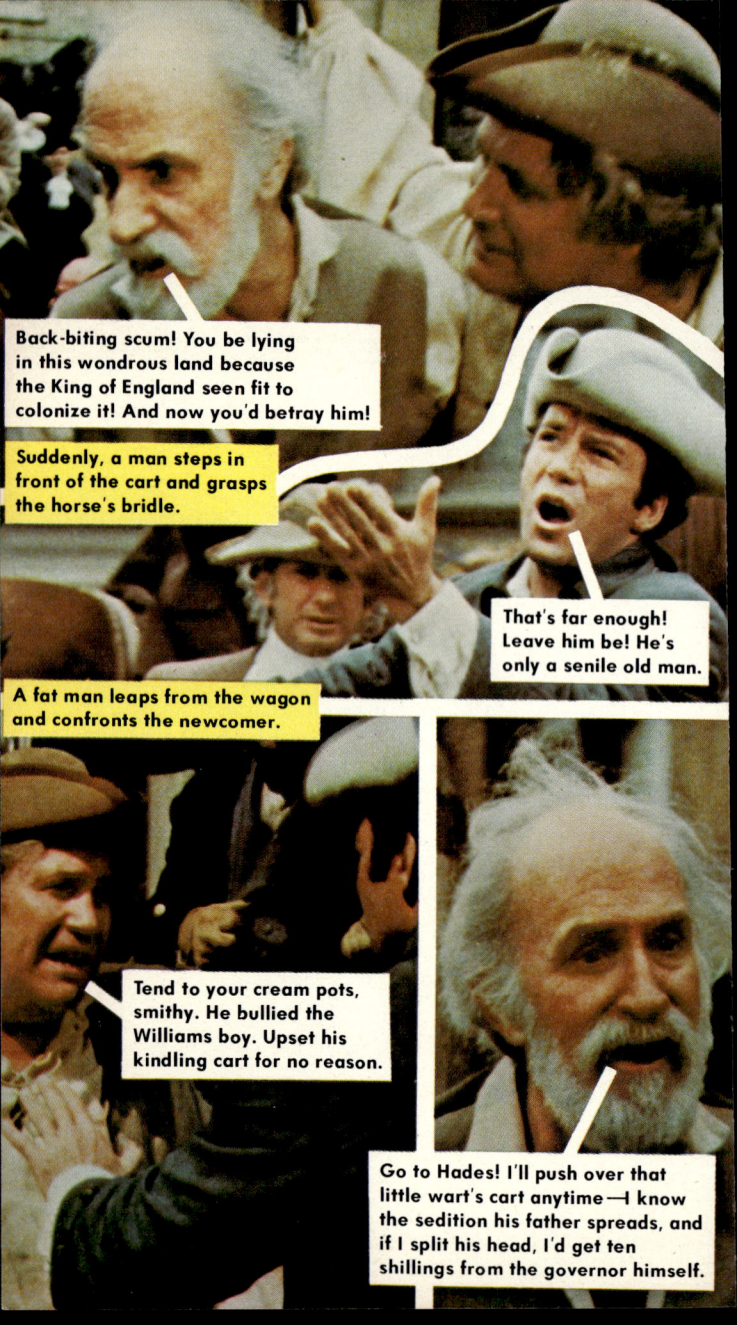

Back-biting scum! You be lying in this wondrous land because the King of England seen fit to colonize it! And now you'd betray him!

Suddenly, a man steps in front of the cart and grasps the horse's bridle.

That's far enough! Leave him be! He's only a senile old man.

A fat man leaps from the wagon and confronts the newcomer.

Tend to your cream pots, smithy. He bullied the Williams boy. Upset his kindling cart for no reason.

Go to Hades! I'll push over that little wart's cart anytime—I know the sedition his father spreads, and if I split his head, I'd get ten shillings from the governor himself.

"If you're a friend of liberty, leave off torturing a helpless enemy. Have you no idea what you do to the cause?"

"You give me cause, sir... for this!"

The fat man heaves himself at the other, but suddenly Philip Kent leaps into the fray and batters the aggressor with well-placed punches.

The crowd wants their sport, and stones begin to fly at Philip and the newcomer, pelting them and driving them back.

The angry mob pushes on, shouting "Tar and feathers" while the mad Malcolm taunts them every step of the way.

Animals! To revel in such savagery. Get a statement out, Ben. Let Boston know the Sons of Liberty had nothing to do with this... and we'll see to those who did.

Edes introduces Philip to the man, Paul Revere, a silversmith who offers to repay Philip for his help by replacing a silver button or two.

I don't have many of those yet, Mr. Revere.

Yet? Spoken like a real Yankee!

...des examines a welt rising on Philip's ...orehead that was caused by a stone ...om the mob.

...n truth, sir, I can't say I'm ...eady to fight for your cause, ...ut I think I understand it.

Now that you've felt the sting of a mob, do you have second thoughts about working with men who incite them to action?

Better than most, I imagine. England looks upon us as her bastard sons, but we feel we're her true sons. Welcome to America, Mr. Kent, and to a common cause.

The weeks pass, and Philip becomes a valuable assistant to his employer. One day, while he is alone in the shop, a pretty, but haughty young girl enters. She is Anne Ware, daughter of a Boston lawyer who is known to oppose British policy in the colony.

This is copy from my father to be set immediately.

Philip scans the paper and nods, saying he agrees with her father's political stand.

"Do you? I wasn't aware an ordinary printer's devil approved or disapproved copy."

Philip, annoyed by her manner, turns away to appear busy, leaving the girl waiting.

"I did address you sharply, but this article is important. As soon as the material is proofed, my father would welcome a message to that effect, if you will so notify Mr. Edes."

"What?"

"Please."

"If you will so notify Mr. Edes, please."

Bested, Anne pauses at the door to cast a glance of agitation at this audacious young man who is not cowed by her beauty.

That night, Philip is invited by Edes to wait on table at the secret meeting of the leaders of the Sons of Liberty in the back room of The <u>Salutation.</u> In the talk that follows, it is clear that Samuel Adams is determined to provoke the people of Boston and Massachusetts Bay to confront the English and demand civil rights.

Confrontation and conflagration will surely come. The sooner the citizens understand and accept that . . .

Abraham Ware supports Adams, although not everyone in the room is so eager for open rebellion.

"We must hammer at them daily, with issues."

Philip is astonished by the passion of these men, who are set on shaking the current order at its very roots to assure the colonials of the same rights as all Englishmen. Dr. Warren is against inciting an uprising.

"Samuel, you are a manipulator! And I will never agree that "conflagration" —your prettified term for open rebellion, for war, is inevitable!"

"Then, sir, you are blind."

The next day, the officer Philip scarred tells Ware he must quarter a Redcoat—Sergeant Lumden.

You must be aware that I conduct a goodly portion of my business from my home. I won't be having strangers about when my clients are here.

We're well acquainted with your business, and with your political persuasion. There will be no breach of faith as long as you keep faith with the Crown. As for strangers, perhaps we could put your mind to rest by permitting me to call on your daughter.

That is an impossibility.

At that moment, Philip arrives, shown in by Daisy, the maid. He carries the proofs of the copy Lawyer Ware requested be set. He and Stark recognize each other.

To irritate Stark, Anne warmly greets Philip and takes his arm. Stark bristles.

Your daughter keeps company with mechanics?

By preference.

Stark prepares to leave, stops and stares at Philip, who returns his harsh look with equal hostility.

Boston is not so large that we won't meet again, mechanic. Good day.

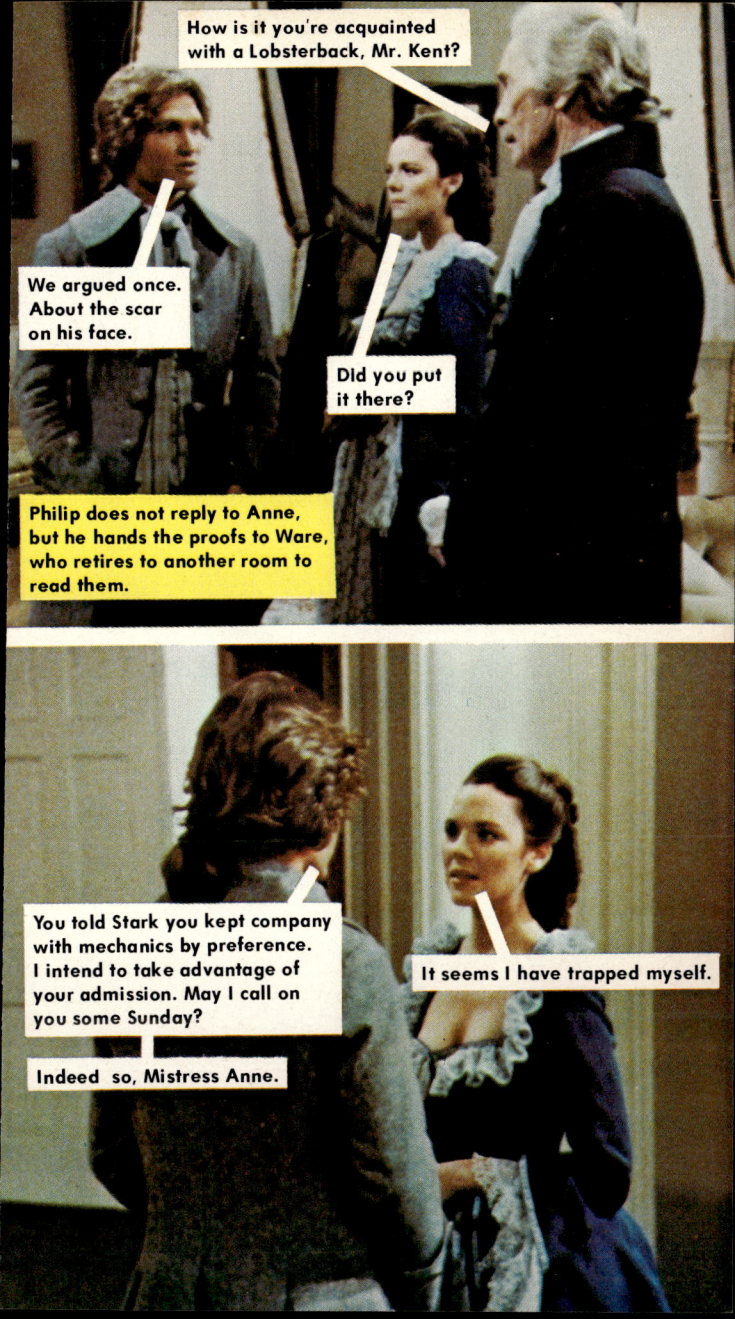

How is it you're acquainted with a Lobsterback, Mr. Kent?

We argued once. About the scar on his face.

Did you put it there?

Philip does not reply to Anne, but he hands the proofs to Ware, who retires to another room to read them.

You told Stark you kept company with mechanics by preference. I intend to take advantage of your admission. May I call on you some Sunday?

It seems I have trapped myself.

Indeed so, Mistress Anne.

That Sunday, Anne and Philip row to a secluded spot.

They stroll and talk about rising discontent in the colonies. Their talk turns to other matters, until Anne tells Philip...

There's more to living than having babies. I intend one day to take part in my husband's work... when I... know who he is.

The attraction between them at that moment is overwhelming, and Philip gently kisses her. But the kiss will go no further, for Anne pulls away.

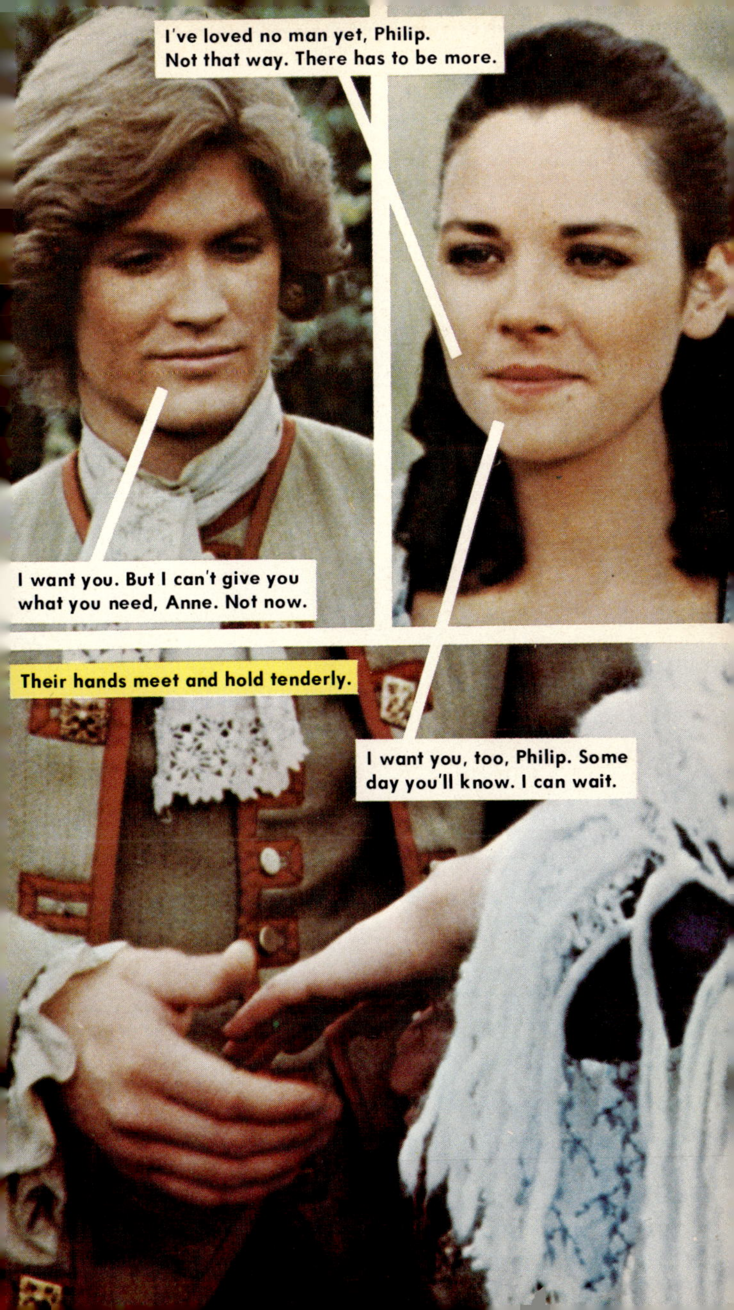

I've loved no man yet, Philip. Not that way. There has to be more.
I want you. But I can't give you what you need, Anne. Not now.
Their hands meet and hold tenderly.
I want you, too, Philip. Some day you'll know. I can wait.

That evening, three men set the Edes Printing House ablaze...

...and dash away just as Philip arrives...

...to raise the alarm and battle the fire. Joined by passersby, Philip saves the shop from destruction.

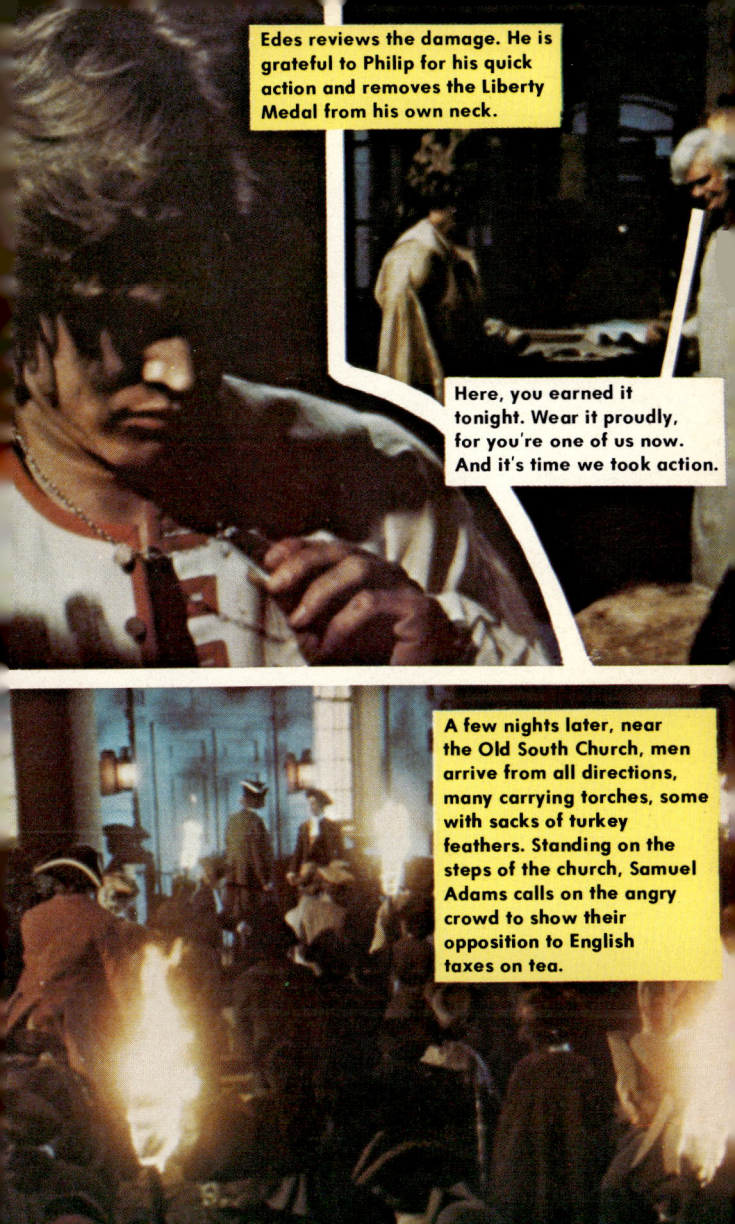

> Edes reviews the damage. He is grateful to Philip for his quick action and removes the Liberty Medal from his own neck.

> Here, you earned it tonight. Wear it proudly, for you're one of us now. And it's time we took action.

> A few nights later, near the Old South Church, men arrive from all directions, many carrying torches, some with sacks of turkey feathers. Standing on the steps of the church, Samuel Adams calls on the angry crowd to show their opposition to English taxes on tea.

Listening to Adams on the edge of the crowd is Philip Kent.

... we have but one choice! To find out how well tea mingles with seawater. Let's brew some tea!

There is an eager shout from the crowd, and the men, many of them wrapped in blankets and bedecked with feathers to look like Indians, surge away toward the wharves.

Standing nearby with her father, Anne Ware watches one of the angry assemblage —Philip Kent.

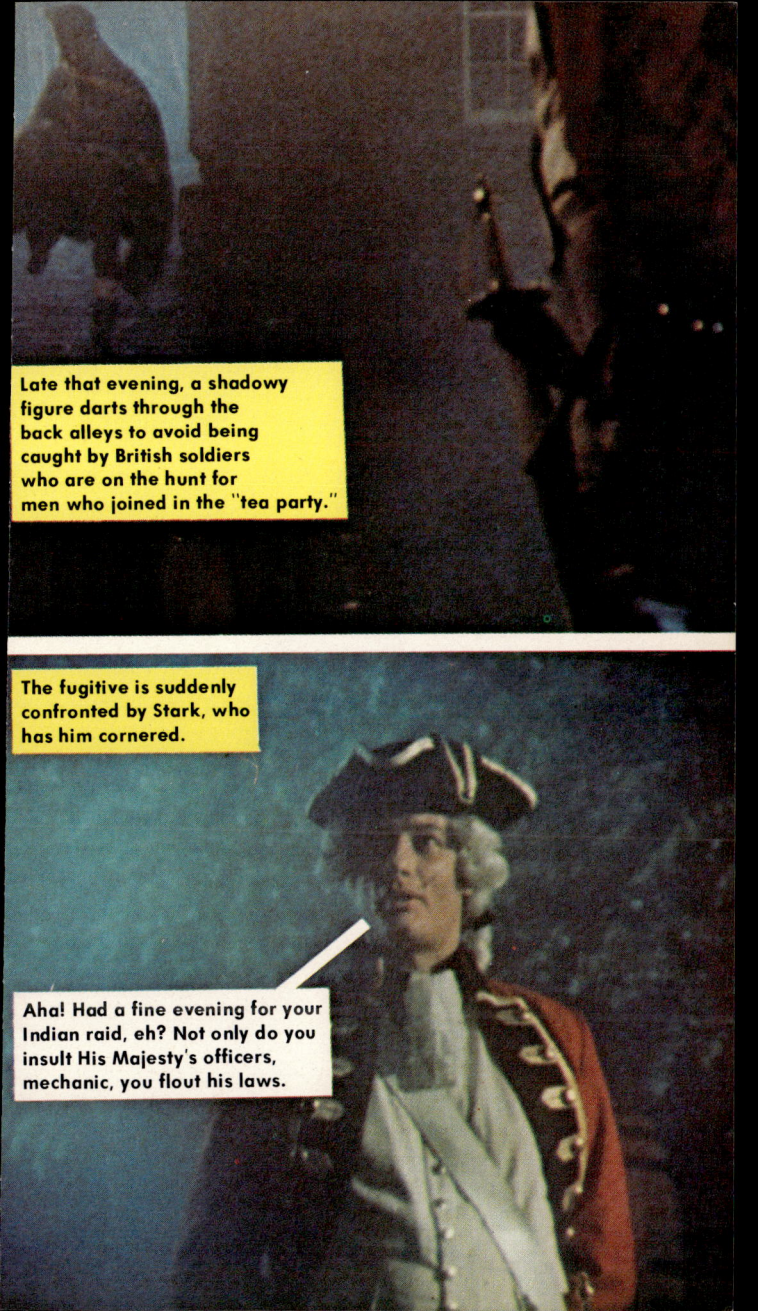

Late that evening, a shadowy figure darts through the back alleys to avoid being caught by British soldiers who are on the hunt for men who joined in the "tea party."

The fugitive is suddenly confronted by Stark, who has him cornered.

Aha! Had a fine evening for your Indian raid, eh? Not only do you insult His Majesty's officers, mechanic, you flout his laws.

Stark draws and thrusts at his unarmed victim.

While you're rotting here, I'll call on the young lady again. Remember that while you're bleeding to death!

The wounded Philip lunges desperately at Stark, toppling him backwards, and the sword clatters to the ground.

Stark leaps to his feet... but Philip has the sword now, and the officer is impaled on his own weapon.

A dazed Philip, bleeding from a slash on his ribs, stumbles off into the night.

He arrives at the printing house and fumbles at the lock. When a hand grasps him from behind, he whirls in fury.

Anne!

I saw you go... I thought what could happen. I had to... Philip!

She feels the blood on his shirt.

It's nothing, let go....

I won't leave you like this. Inside, Philip!

They enter the print shop.

Anne gently bathes and bandages Philip's shallow wound.

Oh, Philip, all I could think about when I saw you leave tonight was how I've been prattling on about the future, and we may not have any future at all.

As Anne dims the lamp, the weary Philip remains silent.

Tonight I knew what I had to do ... to come here and say what I've never said to anyone before.

I want you Philip. With no conditions. No promises. No pledges about tomorrow.

She comes to him, slowly unbuttons her bodice, and ...

I want you, Philip. Even if it's only for this one night.

A drum beats cadence as a rag-tag group of militiamen carrying stout sticks instead of muskets drill across a mowed field, preparing for the trouble that seems more inevitable every passing day.

Among them is Philip Kent, who is taken aside by commander Henry Knox, who tells him he will make a good soldier. But their talk is interrupted by a boy who brings a message.

Damn them to hell! New bill passed in Parliament.... The Province of Massachusetts is to be punished for destroying the tea....

That night, in **The Salutation**, the message is read by Lawyer Ware.

...as well as for her long and open rebelliousness against Crown authority in general. The bill forbids loading or unloading of cargo in Boston Harbor.

The eventual outcome, if the ministers dare to continue sponsoring such laws, will be united resistance, and then...

Independence!

A stony silence weighs heavily in the room as the men consider that prospect, a prospect that has been on all of their minds.

> Revere breaks the mood and says...

> I've speculated who among us would be the first to speak that word.

> I will accept nothing else.

Anne reads a letter her father sent from Philadelphia where representatives of the thirteen colonies are planning to make their case known to Parliament.

". . . to hear such gentlemen as the very respected Colonel Washington of Virginia voice the same concerns as the men of Boston — that, my dearest daughter, is an experience not capable of being fully described . . . ."

Your father's a good man. Does he say when he might return to Boston?

No. Thankfully. As much as I miss him, I think I'd miss this time alone even more.

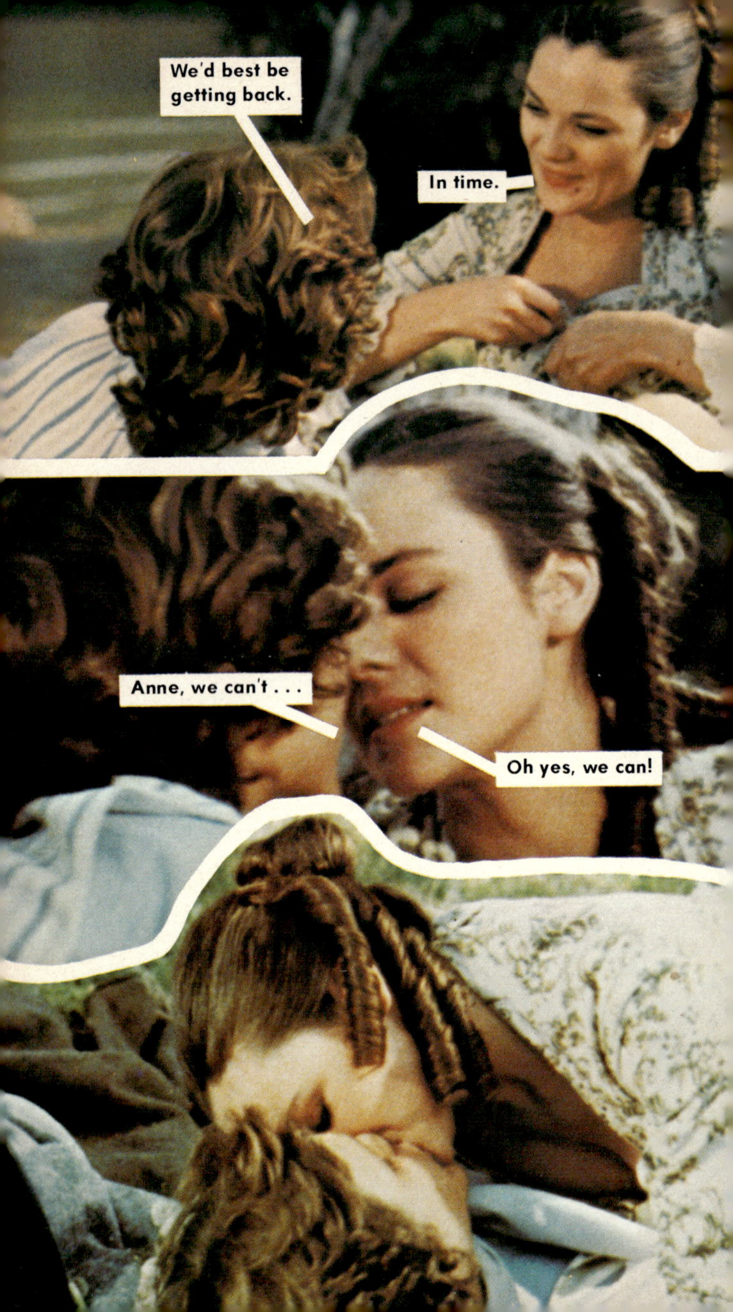
We'd best be getting back.
In time.
Anne, we can't . . .
Oh yes, we can!

On returning home, Anne and Philip surprise Daisy and Sergeant Lumden.

"Oh! Miss Anne, oh!"

Lumden scrambles to his feet, clumsily pulling on his trousers while Daisy quickly covers up.

"Don't think ill of Daisy, Mistress Ware! It was me made her —I mean . . . oh, damn!"

"I just don't know what got into us . . . I mean into me! I just took complete advantage of the poor girl. . . ."

"It's all right."

Daisy, forgive me! Please, forgive me!
Oh, George! Get up!
Truth is, Mistress Ware, I've been wanting to talk to you for some time now, if I can speak in confidence.
Of course you can, Sergeant.
That's it. The sergeant part. That's what's wrong between us . . . the blasted army. I'm going to leave it.
My father has a farm near Concord. George can hide there.
My feelings for Daisy have changed my attitude about everything. We're going to be married

What about your musket?
Musket?
Your musket and bayonet. That's my price for seeing you safely to Concord.
It's yours.

We'll dress as farmers. We'll need a horse and cart. I can talk to Mr. Campbell at The Salutation, see if he can help us. I'd say five shillings should do it.

That evening, at **The Salutation**, the boy Jeremy accepts a bribe from two English officers in exchange for information about Sergeant Lumden.

He's quartered at Mr. Ware's house. Mr. Campbell's gettin' a cart for him an' Mr. Kent....

Kent? The traitor calls himself Kent? Describe him!

Jeremy tells what he knows about Philip. The officer is Roger Amberly, who is sure it is his half brother.

I'll deal with this alone, Major. It's time that both our troops and the citizens of Boston learn the price of betrayal. I intend this incident to become a lesson... and I shall teach it personally.

Later, Amberly's horse stands waiting outside the Ware house, where...

... Philip and Lumden fear discovery of their plan.

"An officer inside with Mistress Anne! They know!"

In the house, Roger presses Anne about Philip. His leering interrogation becomes threatening.

"Get out!"

"Your lover has a way with women. My wife was his lover, too. Did he tell you about her?"

"Perhaps when he learns what sweet pleasures I've taken here, he'll be as eager to seek his revenge as I am mine...."

Roger roughly kisses Anne and throws her on the couch.

Anne screams.

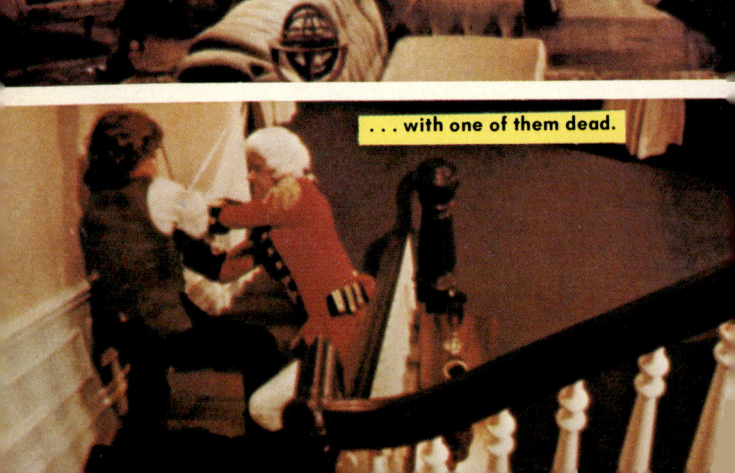

The door crashes open and Philip, sword drawn, faces Roger.

"Outside! I won't spill your blood in this house."

"Charboneau. You dare to take the name Kent!"

"I wrote Alicia about finding you. And about your long-overdue death!"

Steel clashes and the half brothers begin the duel that can end in only one way...

...with one of them dead.

... Philip and Lumden fear discovery of their plan.

"An officer inside with Mistress Anne! They know!"

In the house, Roger presses Anne about Philip. His leering interrogation becomes threatening.

"Get out!"

"Your lover has a way with women. My wife was his lover, too. Did he tell you about her?"

"Perhaps when he learns what sweet pleasures I've taken here, he'll be as eager to seek his revenge as I am mine...."

Roger roughly kisses Anne and throws her on the couch.

Anne screams.

The door crashes open and Philip, sword drawn, faces Roger.

Outside! I won't spill your blood in this house.

Charboneau. You dare to take the name Kent!

I wrote Alicia about finding you. And about your long-overdue death!

Steel clashes and the half brothers begin the duel that can end in only one way...

...with one of them dead.

Roger is overeager to slay Philip, whose blade finds an opening, ending their rivalry, forever.

Your . . . brother?

He was many things to me. But never a brother.

If anyone comes for him, he never arrived. You never saw him, never heard his name before.

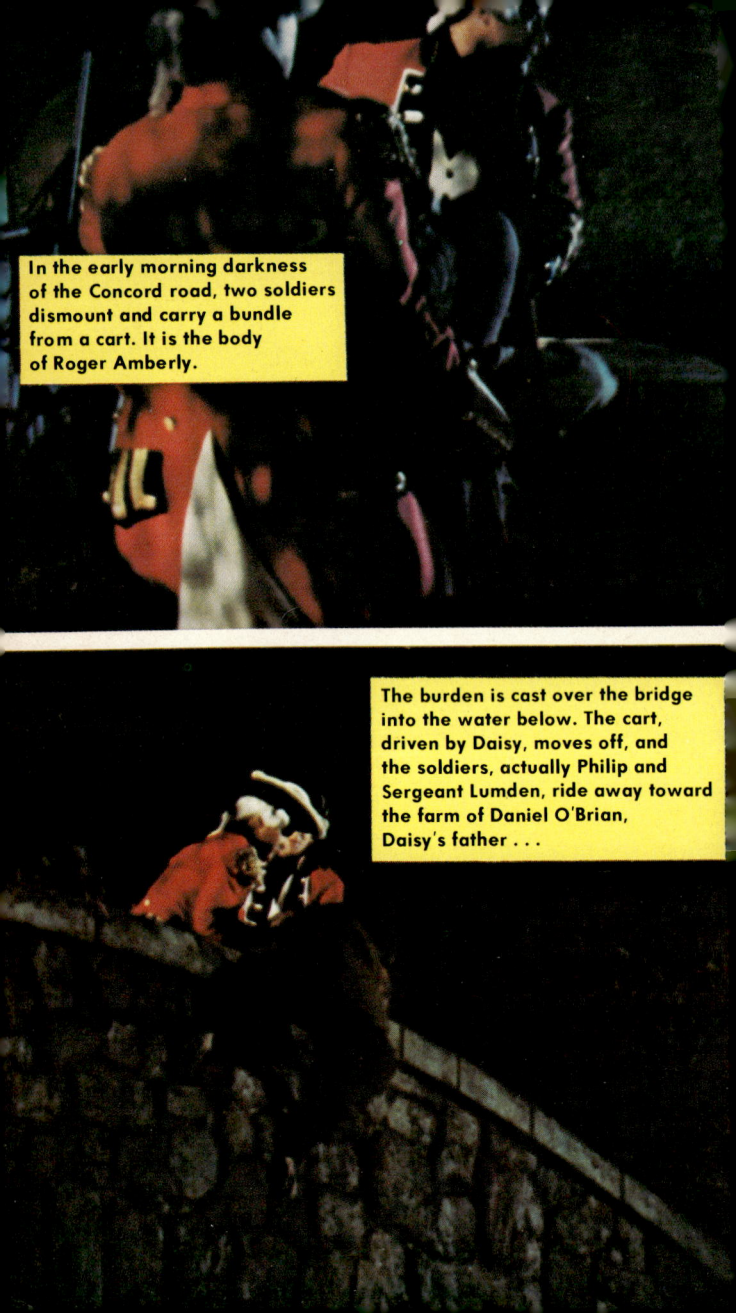

In the early morning darkness of the Concord road, two soldiers dismount and carry a bundle from a cart. It is the body of Roger Amberly.

The burden is cast over the bridge into the water below. The cart, driven by Daisy, moves off, and the soldiers, actually Philip and Sergeant Lumden, ride away toward the farm of Daniel O'Brian, Daisy's father . . .

... where they are greeted by two men who despise the red coats they are wearing and show it by firing warning shots.

One is Lucas, who fought alongside Philip against Plummer. He recognizes Philip, but it is difficult to convince Daisy's father. The suspicious O'Brian finally relents.

Later, he is astonished to learn of Lumden's plan to marry his daughter.

At last, O'Brian accepts even this startling news.

Since you'll be stayin', we must waste no time installin' you in the Concord militia. And we can use those coats for target practice!

A few days later, Colonel James Barrett, the leader of the Concord Militia, tells his volunteers that the Colonial Provincial Congress in Philadelphia has put the militia troops on notice.

There seems little doubt that we are but weeks away from war. Any of you not ready in heart and mind to accept open confrontation with His Majesty's Grenadiers best tell me now.

Gloom overshadows the men, but none speak. The company is dismissed for the day.

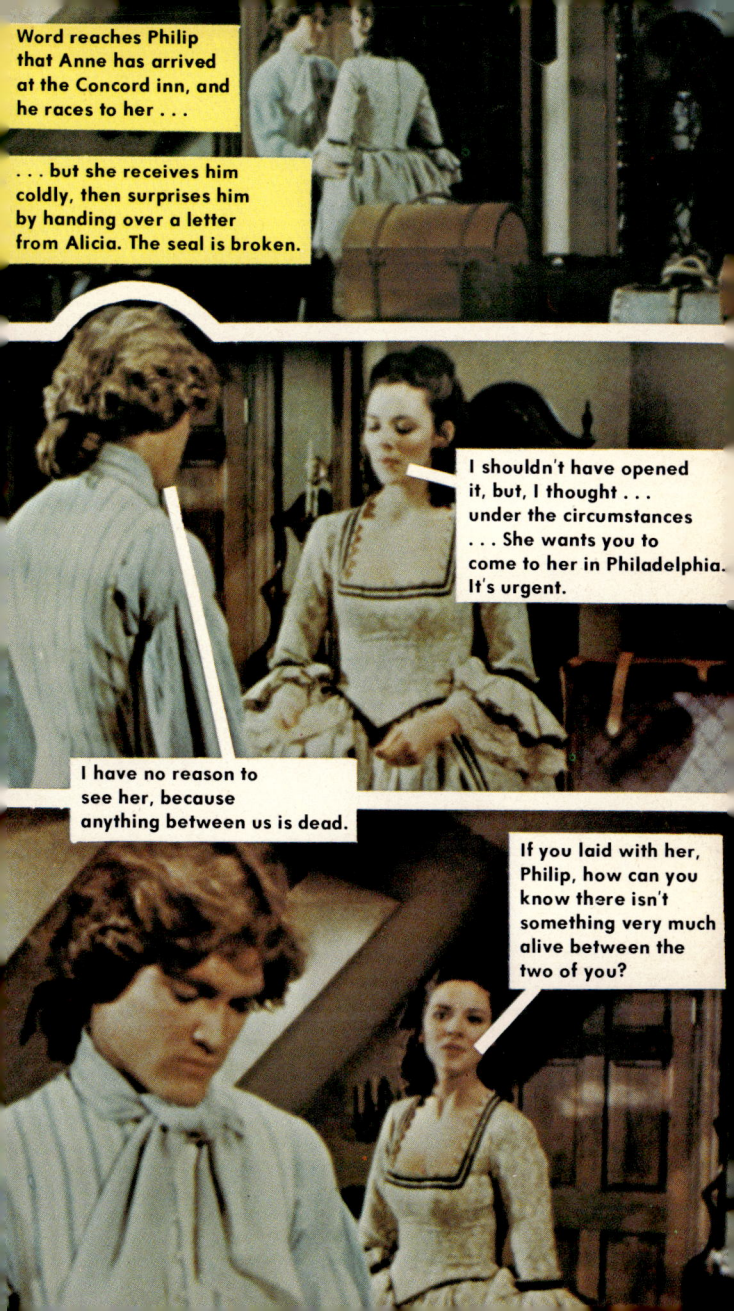

Word reaches Philip that Anne has arrived at the Concord inn, and he races to her...

...but she receives him coldly, then surprises him by handing over a letter from Alicia. The seal is broken.

I shouldn't have opened it, but, I thought... under the circumstances... She wants you to come to her in Philadelphia. It's urgent.

I have no reason to see her, because anything between us is dead.

If you laid with her, Philip, how can you know there isn't something very much alive between the two of you?

"A child? Does she say that?"

"No. But you don't deny it's possible. You don't deny you took her the way he said you did. Why, Philip? Because you had to have everything that belonged to him?"

"Anne, stop it!"

"You still want those dreams your mother spun for you! You want everything your brother had—even his wife!"

The words sting, but Philip will not counter.

"Anne, I've gone through most of my life not knowing who I am. If I have fathered a child . . . that child will never know the doubts I've known."

She is reluctant to kiss him, and he leaves. Alone, Anne surrenders to her sadness.

Philadelphia.

Philip Kent rides to the City Tavern, where the letter said Alicia would await him.

He is astonished to be led to magnificent rooms, where...

...the still-lovely Alicia appears and is somehow in his arms once more.

Oh, Phillipe, hold me! Hold me! You're really here, and there's nothing to keep us apart!

The familiar scent, the overwhelming sensation of Alicia's body close...

...but he pulls away.

You? I might have guessed.

...parently there's ...mething you ...n't know. I ...ed Roger.

...cia, I have to know ...have there been children?

Children? No, Phillipe, you've fathered no children yet... at least none that I know of. Is there anyone else in particular?

Yes. She's waiting for me now.

When it comes to waiting, Master Frenchman, I'm at the head of the line.

Phillipe, you were born to share my bed. All the dreams, they're not dreams any more, they're real.

...nd Philip is swept away ... Alicia's passion...

Alicia.

In the weeks that follow, the wealth of Philadelphia is at Philip's feet, and...

A suit in that color also.

But I'll never wear them all.

Never twice. A man in your position doesn't have to wear them twice, darling.

... the sensuous Alicia is in his arms.

One sunny morning Philip encounters Dr. Franklin, who admires the young man's success and asks for news of Boston, where events are moving rapidly in the city's open opposition to the government.

We are denied our heritage by a Crown that refuses to recognize us as her rightful sons. If only Parliament would stand up to German George, but they won't. Not North, not Dartmouth not Kentland...

You said "Kentland?"

Aye, James Amberly, assistant secretary for overseas affairs....

The shattered Philip learns that the duke is alive. He has been deceived by even his lover, Alicia.

Damn them! Damn them to hell!

Don't hate them all, Philip. Not your father. I have a bastard son myself, but I love him none the less for his illegitimacy.

"My mother died because of them."

"It can't be easy for any of us. But it may be necessary to survive... to know who we are...."

Philip digests the words, then returns to the inn. Alicia is waiting.

"Was it as easy the first time, Alicia? The wreath on the door, the show of grief? Was it as easy to buy all that as it's been to buy me?"

"Then you found out! Oh, so glad! I didn't know how to tell you... and you don't hate me?"

"Hate you? The pieces of my life have finally fallen into place. How can I hate you for helping that to happen?"

He won't honor that now. Not when he learns how Roger died.
Then we can go to London together? With the letter.
Alicia is startled by Philip's grim manner.
The letter nearly destroyed me.
You still have it, don't you? You didn't destroy it?
Phillipe, tell me the truth!
The truth, dear beautiful Alicia, is that I am a fool. And you . . . are a whore.
Phillipe!
Not Phillipe —Philip.
He leaves Alicia forever, and . . .

... rides rapidly for Concord and Anne Ware. As he arrives, men are gathering, preparing for an expected confrontation with the British the next day. Colonel Barrett is mustering his militia.

British troops are on the road to Concord. Get your muskets, and reassemble as quickly as you can. Now, set to!

Philip hurries to the house where Anne is living. He is met by a somber Lawyer Ware.

Leave her be! She says there's nothing more between you.

Ware implies that Anne is pregnant.

The lawyer prevents Philip's advance by drawing a pistol.

A child? Mr. Ware, I have to see her!

I'll use this, Kent, if you ever try to see her again.

A dismayed Philip is rooted to the spot until Colonel Barrett orders him to mount and spread the alarm.

On the highway, he nearly collides with Paul Revere, Doctor Prescott and William Dawes.

"There's a major advance on Concord to seize military stores. We're riding to give the alarm."

Suddenly, mounted Redcoats appear...

...and cut off escape...

...surrounding the colonial horsemen.

The officer suspects the men are alerting militia.

Turn your horses about, and we'll question you at our Headquarters nearby. If your replies are not truthful, I'll shoot you down.

The riders canter across a stream bed. When the moment is right, Philip smashes a fist into the face of his guard, starting a melee...

...that gives the colonials a chance to break for freedom.

Unhorsed Redcoats shout and fire at the American riders as they dash away unscathed.

Philip returns to the O'Brian farm where his friends are arming themselves and preparing to fight. He stops Daisy...

In case we don't return, tell Anne she has my love.

God bless you, sir.

Alone in the farmhouse, Philip gazes briefly at the Amberly letter. He kneels and places the letter and his mother's jewel box in the fire.

The officer suspects the men are alerting militia.

Turn your horses about, and we'll question you at our Headquarters nearby. If your replies are not truthful, I'll shoot you down.

The riders canter across a stream bed. When the moment is right, Philip smashes a fist into the face of his guard, starting a melee...

...that gives the colonials a chance to break for freedom.

Unhorsed Redcoats shout and fire at the American riders as they dash away unscathed.

Philip returns to the O'Brian farm where his friends are arming themselves and preparing to fight. He stops Daisy...

In case we don't return, tell Anne she has my love.

God bless you, sir.

Alone in the farmhouse, Philip gazes briefly at the Amberly letter. He kneels and places the letter and his mother's jewel box in the fire.

Lucas enters.

Sar, what you do there?

I'm buying my freedom. Living in bondage to another person's principles is the greatest crime a man can commit, Lucas. A crime that destroys his own identity.

Philip slowly stands, and they prepare to leave.

I thought you might want this coat.

You won't need it?

A man doesn't need more than one coat at a time, sar.

No . . . no, he doesn't.

As Philip departs on his new mission, his past lies among the flames to which he consigned it.

Outside, Philip is about to mount along with Lucas and O'Brian when a galloping rider appears.

It is Anne.

The Redcoats are gathering at the bridge. Our militia is forming to hold the line there.

Philip helps her dismount and pulls her close.

Oh, Annie, I tried to see you. Why did you let me go?

You had to go. I couldn't tell you about the baby because I couldn't use that to hold you.

"I love you, Anne. I love you!"

"Men may die today... God knows what sort of a future any of us have, but if you'll still have me..."

"Yes, Philip, yes!"

A relieved Philip quickly mounts and Anne watches proudly as he rides away.

Philip Kent. One of a rare breed of men. Free-spirited individuals who called themselves Americans...

...and marched together to create a nation that would guarantee life, liberty and the pursuit of happiness.